George and Martha, tons of fun
Marshall, James   Test#: 43671
Points: 0.5   Lvl: 2.4

W9-AYW-834

Lincoln School Library

FOR MAURICE SENDAK

Library of Congress Cataloging in Publication Data

Marshall, James, 1942-
  George and Martha, tons of fun.

  SUMMARY: Five brief episodes reveal the ups and
downs of a great friendship.
  [1. Friendship — Fiction. 2. Hippopotamus — Fiction]
I. Title.
PZ7.M35672Gf   [E]   80-13592
ISBN 0-395-29524-6

Copyright © 1980 by James Marshall

All rights reserved. For information about permission
to reproduce selections from this book, write to
Permissions, Houghton Mifflin Company, 215 Park Avenue
South, New York, New York 10003.

Printed in the United States of America

RNF   ISBN   0-395-29524-6
PAP   ISBN   0-395-42646-4

WOZ 20 19 18 17 16

George was practicing his handstands.

"This calls for concentration," he said.

Suddenly the doorbell rang.

It was Martha.

"I've come to chat," she said.

"Not this afternoon," said George.

"I want to be alone."

"I hope Martha understands," said George.

But Martha did not understand.

Martha was offended.

Martha was hurt.

And Martha was *mad!*

A few minutes later, George's telephone rang.

It was Martha.

"George," she said, "I never want to see you again!"

And she slammed down the receiver.

"Oh dear," said George.

Martha was mad all afternoon and evening.

Finally she got out her saxophone.

"This will calm me down," she said.

Soon Martha was having quite a bit of fun.

In fact she was having *so* much fun that she

didn't even answer her telephone.

"Oh dear," said George. "Màrtha must still

be upset."

But Martha had forgotten all about the

misunderstanding.

George had a sweet tooth.

He just couldn't stop himself from eating sweets.

"You know what they say about too much sugar," said Martha.

"Let's not discuss it," said George.

Late at night George would raid the refrigerator to satisfy his sweet tooth.

"You'll weigh a ton," said Martha.

"Let's not discuss it," said George.

"This calls for action!" said Martha.

And she lighted up a cigar.

"Stop that!" cried George. "You'll make yourself sick!"

"Let's not discuss it," said Martha.

"You'll ruin your teeth!" cried George.

"We won't discuss it," said Martha.

"Please!!" cried George. "You're ruining your health."

"No discussion," said Martha.

Martha began to turn a peculiar color.

George couldn't stand it any longer,

and he fell to his knees.

"I'll do anything you say!" he begged.

"Will you cut down on your sweets?"

said Martha.

"I promise," said George.

And Martha put out her cigar.

One day Martha stepped into a
photography booth.
"I love to have my picture taken,"
she said.
"Click," went the camera.

When Martha saw her photograph,
she was thrilled.
"I've never looked prettier," she said.

George was trying to hypnotize Martha.

"Your eyes are getting heavy," said George.

"I believe they are," said Martha.

"You are getting sleepy," said George.

"That's true," said Martha.

And in a moment Martha seemed sound asleep.

"Success!" whispered George.

Ever so quietly George tiptoed to the kitchen,
where he kept his cookie jar.

"Ah-ha!" cried Martha.

George was ashamed.

He'd broken his promise.

"Would you like a cookie?" he asked Martha.

"Yes, I would!" she said.

And she ate them all.

THE LAST STORY

THE SPECIAL GIFT

It was George's birthday, and Martha stopped by the bookshop to buy a gift. "He loves to read," Martha told the salesperson.

On the way to George's house,
Martha played a tricky game of
hopscotch.

George could hardly wait for his gift.

"I can't stand the suspense," he said.

But when Martha went to look for George's book, it wasn't there.

"I'm waiting," said George.

"What will I do?" said Martha to herself.

"I'm waiting," said George.

Martha quickly decided to give George
the photograph of herself.
"It's not much," she said.
When George saw Martha's picture,
he fell off his chair laughing.
"*Well!*" said Martha. "What's so funny?"

"This is the best gift I've ever received,"
  said George.

"It *is*?" said Martha.

"Of course," said George. "It's wonderful to have
  a friend who knows how to make you laugh."
  Martha decided to swallow her pride.
  She saw that the photograph was pretty funny
  after all.

E
MAR

Marshall, James,

George and Martha,
tons of fun

DATE DUE			
MAY 2 2 '06			
APR 0 4 2007			
APR 3 0 2008			
APR 2 0 2009			

Lincoln School Library